GOD MAKES BEAUTIFUL THINGS

Written by
Karen L. Nourse

Illustrated by
Antim Marius

Author: Karen L. Nourse
Illustrator: Antim Marius

ISBN Paper Book: 978-0-578-51224-2
Library of Congress Control Number: 2020906384

Karen L. Nourse
Publisher
KarLynn111@gmail.com

Printed and bound in the United States

This book is dedicated to all of God's children

To: Aeva + Ellie

Karen Nourse

I love flowers.
Flowers make
me happy.

I love the sun.
It warms my face.

"What are you doing, little kitty?"
asked the puppy.

"I'm enjoying the things that God has made," said the kitty.

"Who is God?"

"God is our Father in heaven.
He loves us and watches over us,"
said the kitty.

"Come with me, and I'll show you some of the things that God has made," said the kitty.

"Look at the spider in its web," said the kitty. "God made that spider."

"This pond has baby tadpoles swimming in it," said the kitty. "When they grow up, they'll become big green frogs."

"There goes a mommy racoon with her furry babies," said the kitty.

"I see an owl sleeping in that big oak tree," whispered the kitty.

"Hello, little bird. You're so tiny."

"What's that noise I hear?"

"It's a waterfall," said the kitty. "Let's get closer to it."

"I love rainbows," yelled the kitty.

"Yes, He did," said the kitty.

"God can do anything!" shouted the puppy. "I want to be His friend."

"All you have to do is ask Him, and He will be your friend forever."

"I'll do that," said the puppy, with a thump, thump, thump of his tail.

"I have to go home now," sighed the puppy.

"Before you go, I have something special to show you," said the kitty.

"God made you and me," said the kitty.

"He made me?"

"Yes, He made you," said the kitty.

"God's the best!" said the puppy.

"Will you show me more things that God has made when I come back to visit with you?" asked the puppy.

"Of course, I will. There's so much more to see," said the kitty.

"Goodbye, sweet puppy," said the kitty.

"Goodbye, little kitty," said the puppy. "Thank you for showing me some of the beautiful things God has made."

God's Love

God's love is like a warm gentle breeze
God's love is like a hug filled with affection
God's love is like a kiss from someone you cherish
God's love is like a helping hand to someone in need
God's love is like a baby that has been rocked to sleep
God's love is like a father who loves his children
God's love is like a friend who always listens
God's love is like a cozy blanket
God's love is like a kind word
God's love is always there
God's love never ends
God is love

CPSIA information can be obtained
at www.ICGtesting.com
Printed in the USA
LVHW072231300421
686158LV00002B/6

9 780578 51224